Karma Wilson

Matt Myers

A DOG NAMED DOUG

Margaret K. McElderry Books

New York
London   Toronto
Sydney
New Delhi

Once there was a dog named Doug.
Doug liked to dig, but when Doug dug . . .

oh boy, did Doug DIG!

Once he dug up a ground squirrel's nest.
The feisty squirrel was not impressed!

"I CAN DIG better than you!"

Doug howled with laughter. "Let's see if that's true!"

So they started to race, but Doug dug faster;
he proved that he was the digging master!

With his nose down low, the dirt flew high;
clumps hit the cat as Doug sauntered by.

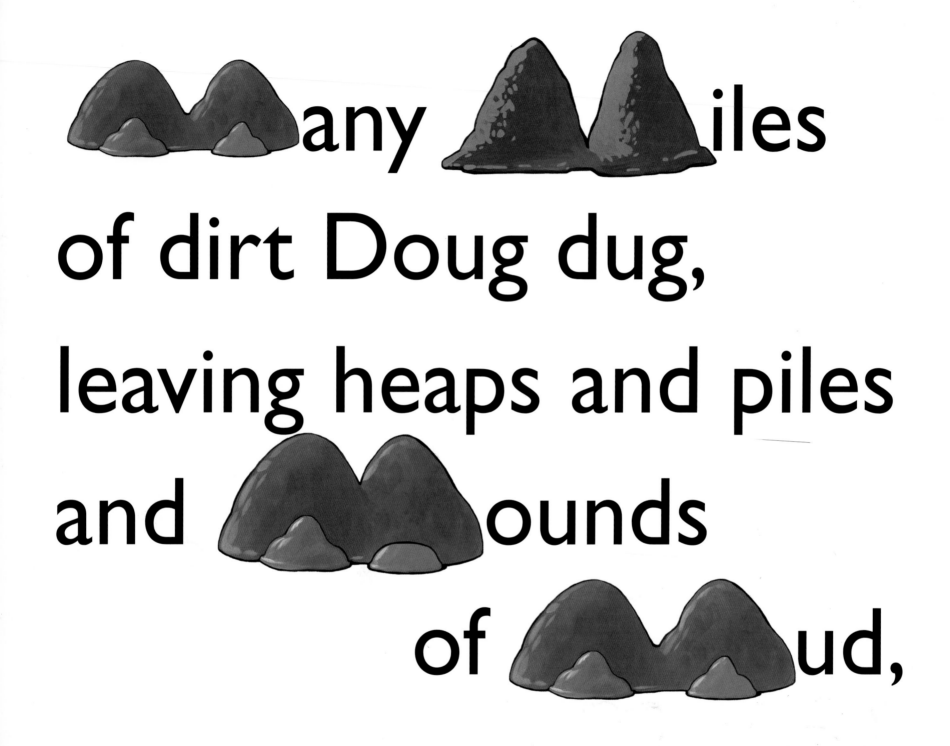

Many Miles
of dirt Doug dug,
leaving heaps and piles
and Mounds
of Mud,

and **ROOTS**

so deep
and holes so wide
that a giant tractor
fell inside!

And boy, did Doug

DIG!

He dug to the

EAST,

he dug to the

WEST.

He dug his way to a treasure chest
with about a million dollars inside!
Doug smiled wide, then tossed it aside.

and took no note of the danger sign.

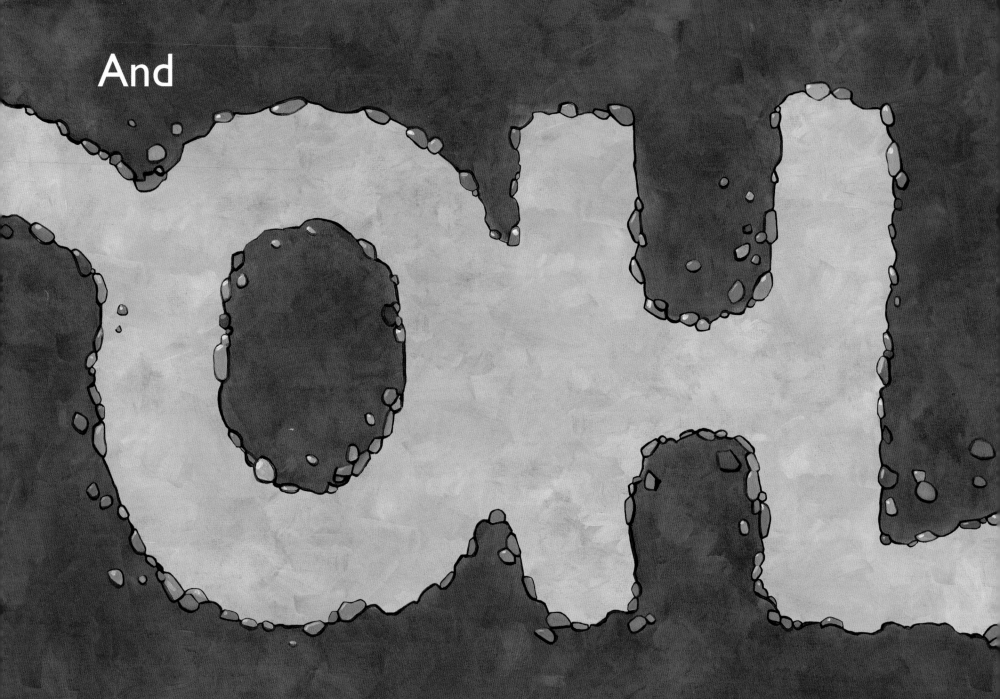

did Doug DIG!

He dug to the

NORTH,

he dug to the

SOUTH.

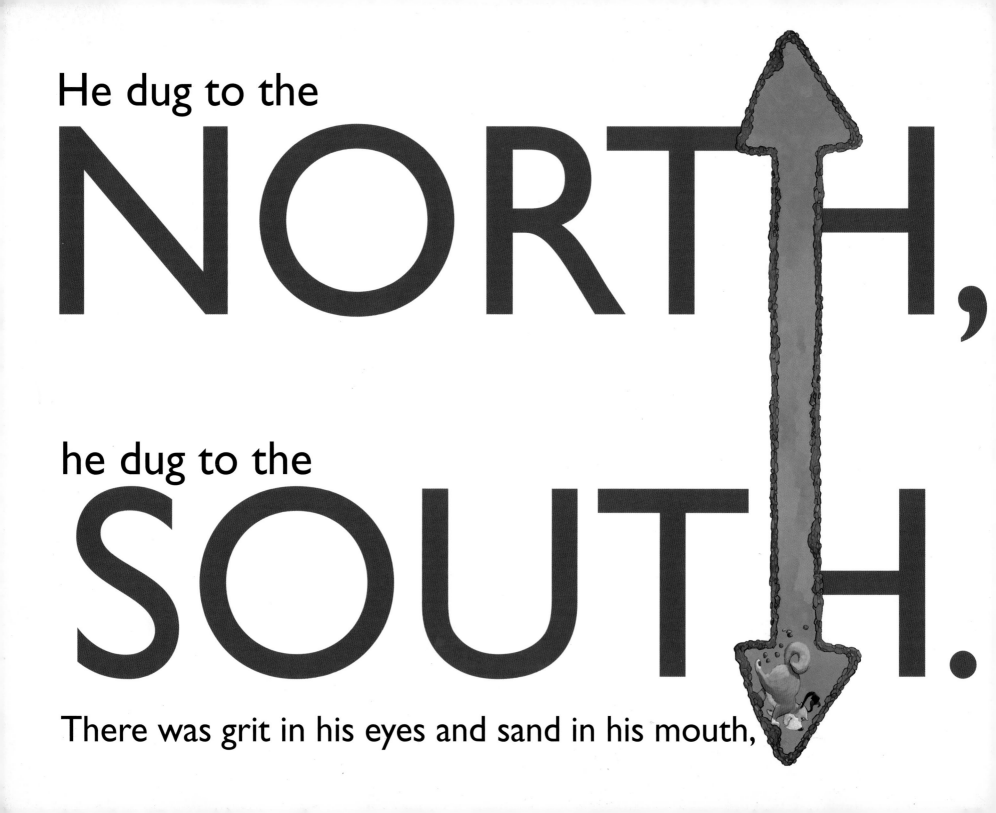

There was grit in his eyes and sand in his mouth,

but Doug kept scratching and scratching on,
till his head popped up on the White House lawn.

He took the tour, he saw the sights,
then decided he'd better dig home for the night.

So Doug got busy digging, and . . .

did Doug DIG!

And dig,

and dig,

and dig,

and dig,

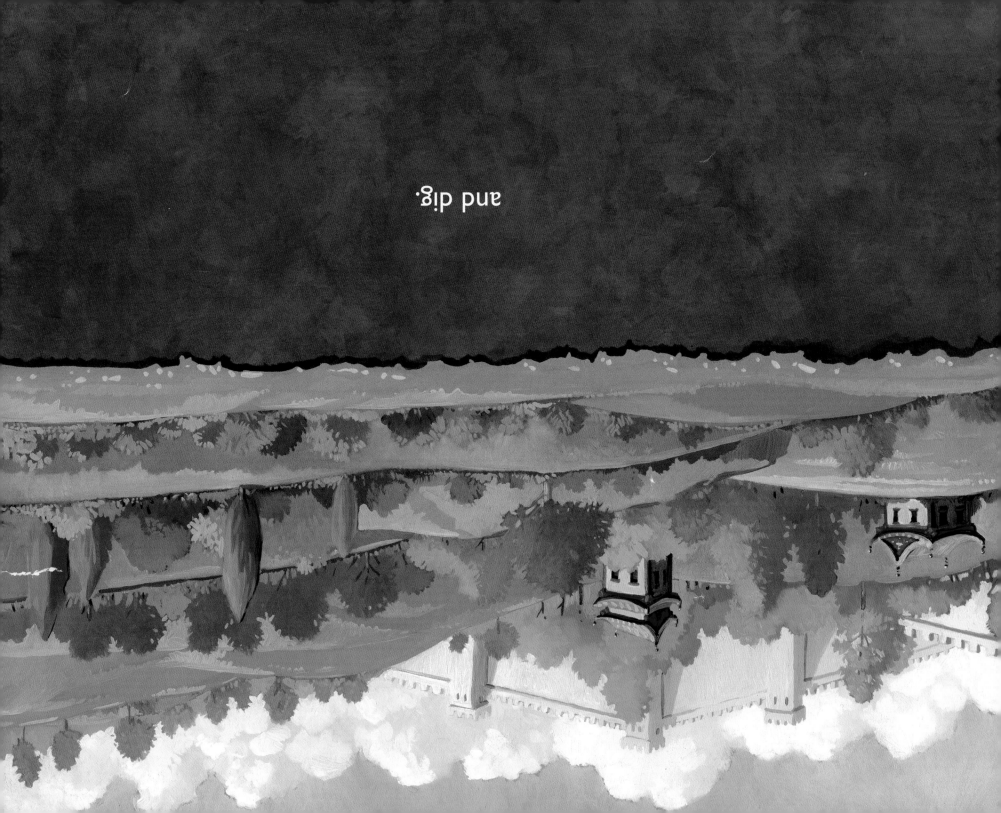

and dig.

At home the family scolded him hard.
"DOUG, STOP DIGGING HOLES IN THE YARD!"

But they fed him a bone, gave him a hug,
then tucked him in bed with a "Good night, Doug!"

But still, Doug

Doug settled in to his cozy bed,
with visions of marvelous holes in his head;
Doug had a dream he was digging!

For my long-lost brothers
and newfound friends, Steve & Scott
All my love, Karma—K.W.

For Justin, who keeps digging
until he gets to the gold—M. M.

MARGARET K. McELDERRY BOOKS • An imprint of Simon & Schuster Children's Publishing Division • 1230 Avenue of the Americas, New York, New York 10020 • Text copyright © 2018 by Karma Wilson • Illustrations copyright © 2018 by Matt Myers • All rights reserved, including the right of reproduction in whole or in part in any form. • MARGARET K. McELDERRY BOOKS is a trademark of Simon & Schuster, Inc. • For information about special discounts for bulk purchases, please contact Simon & Schuster Special Sales at 1-866-506-1949 or business@simonandschuster.com. • The Simon & Schuster Speakers Bureau can bring authors to your live event. For more information or to book an event, contact the Simon & Schuster Speakers Bureau at 1-866-248-3049 or visit our website at www.simonspeakers.com.
Book design by Lauren Rille • The text for this book was set in Gill Sans. • The illustrations for this book were rendered in acrylic and oil paint on illustration board.
Manufactured in China • 0418 SCP • First Edition • 10 9 8 7 6 5 4 3 2 1
Library of Congress Cataloging-in-Publication Data
Names: Wilson, Karma, author. | Myers, Matt, illustrator. | Title: A dog named Doug / Karma Wilson ; illustrated by Matt Myers.
Description: First Edition. | New York : Margaret K. McElderry Books, [2018] | Summary: Egged on by a ground squirrel, a dog named Doug digs miles underground—taking a detour through the White House—until he returns home, goes to bed, and dreams of digging some more. | Identifiers: LCCN 2017013002 (print) | LCCN 2017041285 (ebook) | ISBN 9781442449312 (hardcover) | ISBN 9781442449329 (Ebook) | Subjects: | CYAC: Stories in rhyme. | Dogs—Fiction. | Tunneling—Fiction.
Classification: LCC PZ8.3.W6976 (ebook) | LCC PZ8.3.W6976 DI 2018 (print) | DDC [E]—dc23 | LC record available at https://lccn.loc.gov/2017013002